Ling & Ting

TOGETHER IN ALL WEATHER

by Grace Lin

L B

LITTLE, BROWN AND COMPANY
New York Boston

To Alex,
who has been with me
through all weather

Little, Brown and Company

Hachette Book Group
1290 Avenue of the Americas, New York, NY 10104
Visit us at lb-kids.com

Little, Brown and Company is a division of Hachette Book Group, Inc.
The Little, Brown name and logo are trademarks of Hachette Book Group, Inc.

The publisher is not responsible for websites (or their content)
that are not owned by the publisher.

First Edition: November 2015

Library of Congress Cataloging-in-Publication Data
Lin, Grace, author.
Ling & Ting : together in all weather / by Grace Lin.
pages cm
Summary: Twin sisters Ling and Ting have fun together playing in all kinds of weather.
ISBN 978-0-316-33549-2 (hardcover) 1. Twins—Juvenile fiction. 2. Sisters—Juvenile fiction.
3. Play—Juvenile fiction. 4. Weather—Juvenile fiction. 5. Seasons—Juvenile fiction. [1. Twins—Fiction.
2. Sisters—Fiction. 3. Play—Fiction. 4. Weather—Fiction. 5. Seasons—Fiction.
6. Chinese Americans—Fiction.] I. Title. II. Title: Ling and Ting. III. Title: Together in all weather.
PZ7.L644Lipm 2015   [E]—dc23   2014040293

10 9 8 7 6 5 4 3 2 1

APS

Printed in China

6. Stories

Everyone is here!

I hope we did not forget anything!

Ling and Ting are twins. They live together. They eat together. They play together. They are always together.

They are together when the wind blows. Outside, the sky is dark. The trees sway. The rain falls. There is thunder and lightning.

Lightning flashes. *Crack!*

"Eek!" says Ling.

"Are you scared of the storm?" Ting asks.

"No!" says Ling. "I am not scared! I was just surprised."

Boom! The thunder is loud.

"Eek!" says Ting.

"Are you scared of the storm?" Ling asks.

"No!" Ting says. "I am not scared. I was just surprised, too."

Lightning flashes. *Crack!*

Boom! The thunder is loud.

"Eek!" Ling and Ting say together.

They sit close to each other. They put a blanket over their heads.

"We are not scared," Ling says.

"No," Ting says. "We are just surprised."

Ling and Ting are twins. They are always
together. They are surprised together,
too.

The sun is bright. It is hot.

"Ting," Ling says, "I have an idea. Let us make lemonade. We will sell it. We will make a lot of money."

"Yes!" Ting says. "Let us sell lemonade!"

Ling cuts the lemons. Ting adds the
water, sugar, and ice. They take the
lemonade outside. They take a little box
for money outside, too.

9

The sun is bright. It is hot. No one comes to buy the lemonade. Ling and Ting wait.

"I would like some lemonade," Ting says.

"Ting," Ling says, "the lemonade is for sale. You must buy the lemonade."

Ting buys a glass of lemonade. She gives
Ling a nickel. Ling puts it in the little box.

"Now we have earned a nickel," Ling
says.

"Hmmm," Ting says.

"I would like some lemonade," Ling says.

"You must buy it, too," Ting says.

Ling buys a glass of lemonade. She gives
Ting a nickel.

Ting puts it in the little box with the other nickel.

"Now we have earned two nickels," Ting says.

"Hmmm," Ling says.

"Ling," Ting says, "there are two nickels in the box. We have earned two nickels together."

"Yes," Ling says. "There is one nickel for you and one nickel for me."

"I will take my nickel now," says Ting. She takes one nickel from the box.

"I would like to buy another glass of lemonade," says Ting. She gives Ling the nickel. Ling puts the nickel back into the box.

Then Ting drinks another glass of lemonade. Ling watches her.

"I will take my nickel now, too," says
Ling. She takes a nickel from the box.
Then she gives the nickel to Ting. "I
would like to buy another glass of
lemonade, too."

The sun is bright. It is hot. Ling and Ting buy more lemonade. Ling and Ting drink more lemonade. Soon the lemonade is gone.

"Good job!" Ting says. "We sold all the lemonade!"

"Yes," Ling says. "We did sell all the lemonade. But we did not make a lot of money."

It is cool outside. The leaves are yellow, red, and orange. They are falling from the trees. Ling and Ting are raking leaves.

"Raking is hard work," Ting says. She feels hot. She takes off her hat.

Soon all the leaves are in a big pile.

"We are finished!" Ling says.

Ting nods. Then Ting scratches her head.

"Where is my hat?" Ting asks.

Ting looks for her red hat. Ling helps her.
They look through the big pile of leaves.
Soon there is no pile. They cannot find
the hat.

Then Ling looks at the tree. "Look at that funny red leaf!" says Ling. "It looks like—"

"My hat!" says Ting. "We found my hat!"

Ting is happy. But Ling is not happy. Ling looks at the leaves. There are leaves everywhere. There is no pile of leaves.

"Oops," Ting says. "We must rake again."

Ling nods. Then Ling scratches her head.

"Where is my hat?" Ling asks.

"It is winter," says Ling. "Now we must shovel snow. Ting, let us go shovel the snow."

Ting does not want to shovel the snow. Ting thinks hard. She gets into her bed. She rubs her nose.

"I am sick," Ting says. "I cannot go outside. I cannot shovel the snow."

"You are sick?" Ling asks. "If you are sick, you need medicine. I will make you some."

"You will make me medicine?" Ting asks.

"Yes," Ling says. "I have a recipe. It is for an old Chinese medicine. It works well."

In the kitchen, Ling makes the medicine. She cooks onions, ginger, and water. She adds mustard and garlic. She adds sticks and dirt. She adds a sock and a shoelace. Ting watches from the door.

"Almost done!" Ling says. She stirs the medicine. The medicine looks bad. The medicine smells bad.

"Ling!" Ting says. "I think I am better now. I am not sick. I do not need old Chinese medicine."

"Are you sure?" Ling asks.

"Yes," Ting says. "It is winter. We must shovel snow."

"Good," says Ling. "The old Chinese
medicine really does work well."

The snow is melting. The air is warm. Spring is coming.

"Soon it will be spring," Ling says. "Soon there will be leaves. Soon there will be flowers!"

"Look!" Ting says. "There is already a flower!"

"It is the first flower of spring!" Ling says.
"Let us go see it!"

Ling and Ting go to the flower. They look
at it. Ting scratches her head.

"It is a funny flower!" Ting says. "It looks
like—"

"My hat!" Ling says. "We found my hat!"

"Ling! Look at the strange weather," Ting says. "There is sun and there is rain. There are both at the same time."

"Ting," Ling says, "this is rainbow weather! This is when we can find a rainbow!"

"It is?" Ting asks. "Let us go look for a rainbow! If we find one, we will be lucky!"

Ling looks behind the house. She does not see a rainbow.

Ting looks in front of the house. She does not see a rainbow.

"I looked behind the house," Ling tells Ting. "I did not find a rainbow."

"I looked in front of the house," Ting tells Ling. "I did not find a rainbow, either."

"Let us go to the big hill," Ling says. "We will look for a rainbow together."

Ling and Ting walk up the big hill. The rain still falls. The sun still shines. When they reach the top of the hill, they look for a rainbow.

"Look, Ting! Look!" Ling shouts. "Two rainbows!"

"They are twin rainbows!" Ting says. "Just like us! We found them together! We are seeing them together! We are so lucky to be together!"

"Yes," Ling says. "We are so lucky to be together."

★ ARTIST'S NOTE ★

The illustrations in this book were painted using Turner Design Gouache on Arches hot-pressed watercolor paper. The color palette was inspired by the sudden appearance of a bright rainbow on a gray, glum day. —*Grace Lin*

★ ABOUT THIS BOOK ★

This book was edited by Alvina Ling and designed by Saho Fujii. The production was supervised by Erika Schwartz, and the production editors were Christine Ma and Barbara Bakowski. This book was printed on 128 gsm Gold Sun matte paper. The text was set in StoneInfITC Medium, and the display type was hand-lettered by the author.

Did they say "encore"?

If you want to see more of us, read our other book "Ling and Ting: Twice as Silly."